CAREER EXPLORATION

Athletic Trainer

by Edward Voeller

Consultant:
Brent L. Arnold, Ph.D., ATC
Assistant Professor
University of Virginia

CAPSTONE BOOKS
an imprint of Capstone Press
Mankato, Minnesota

Capstone Books are published by Capstone Press
P.O. Box 669, 151 Good Counsel Drive, Mankato, Minnesota 56002
http://www.capstone-press.com

Printed in the United States of America.

Library of Congress Cataloging-in-Publication Data
Voeller, Edward A.
   Athletic trainer/by Edward Voeller
   p.cm.—(Career exploration)
   Includes bibliographical references (p. 43) and index.
   Summary: Explains the educational requirements, duties, workplace, salary,
and employment opportunities of the job of athletic trainer.
   ISBN 0-7368-0326-2
   1. Athletic trainers—Juvenile literature. [1. Athletic trainers. 2. Vocational
guidance.] I. Title. II. Series.
RC1210.V64 2000
617.1'027—dc21   99-31160
                                                                            CIP

Editorial Credits
Matt Doeden, editor; Steve Christensen, cover designer; Kia Bielke, illustrator;
   Heidi Schoof, photo researcher

Photo Credits
Index Stock Imagery, 17
International Stock/James Davis, 6; Dusty Willison, 38; Michael Philip
   Manneim, 47
Jerry Millevoi, 14, 18, 22, 25, 36, 41, 44
Skjold Photographs, cover, 9, 28, 31, 35
Unicorn Stock Photos, 10
Uniphoto, 13, 21 (bottom); Uniphoto/Scott Suchman, 21 (top)

Table of Contents

Fast Facts

Career Title	Athletic Trainer
O*NET Number	34058B
DOT Cluster (Dictionary of Occupational Titles)	Professional, technical, and managerial occupations
DOT Number	153.224-010
GOE Number (Guide for Occupational Exploration)	10.02.02
NOC Number (National Occupational Classification-Canada)	5254
Salary Range (U.S. Bureau of Labor Statistics, Human Resources Development Canada, and other industry sources, late 1990s figures)	U.S.: $17,000 to $200,000 Canada: $20,000 to $200,000 (Canadian dollars)
Minimum Educational Requirements	U.S.: bachelor of science degree Canada: bachelor of science degree
Certification/Licensing Requirements	U.S.: mandatory Canada: mandatory

4

Subject Knowledge	Customer and personal service; biology; psychology; medicine and dentistry; therapy and counseling
Personal Abilities/Skills	Use common sense and special medical skills to treat sick or handicapped people; understand technical information from supervisors, charts, reference books, manuals, or labels; use eyes, hands, and fingers with skill; work fast during an emergency; change from one duty to another quickly; follow instructions exactly; record information accurately
Job Outlook	U.S.: average growth Canada: poor
Personal Interests	Humanitarian: interest in helping others with their mental, spiritual, physical, or vocational needs
Similar Types of Jobs	Physical therapist (physiotherapist); occupational therapist; athlete; physician's assistant; coach; referee

Chapter 1

Athletic Trainer

Athletic trainers care for the health of physically active people. They care mainly for athletes. But they also care for anyone who suffers an injury common to athletes.

Athletic trainers help athletes who become hurt playing sports. Athletic trainers treat athletes' injuries. They also help athletes stay in good physical condition. This helps athletes prevent future injuries.

About 20,000 people in North America work as athletic trainers. In Canada, athletic trainers are called athletic therapists.

Immediate Care

Athletic trainers often are the first to help injured athletes. They provide immediate care

Athletic trainers help athletes stay fit and healthy.

for common injuries such as sprains, cuts, and bruises. They also treat more serious injuries such as broken bones and concussions. Hard blows to the head can cause these brain injuries.

Athletic trainers may come onto playing surfaces to provide immediate care. For example, an athletic trainer may rush onto a football field to treat an injured player. Immediate care may include first aid and cardiopulmonary resuscitation (CPR). CPR is a method of treating a heart that has stopped beating.

Athletes sometimes suffer injuries athletic trainers cannot treat. For example, an athlete may suffer a broken neck or back. Athletic trainers call doctors or paramedics when this happens. Athletic trainers help the athletes as much as they can until the doctors or paramedics arrive.

Sprains and Strains

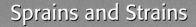

About 60 percent of athletic injuries are sprains or strains. A sprain is an injury to a ligament. These bands of tissue hold bones together. Sprains occur when ligaments stretch too far. Ankle sprains are common among basketball players. Knee sprains are common for soccer and volleyball players. Gymnasts often have wrist and finger sprains.

A strain is an injury to a muscle or tendon. Tendons are bands of tissue that connect muscles to bones. Strains occur when athletes stretch muscles too far. Hamstring strains are common sports injuries. The hamstring muscle is behind the thigh. Football players and runners often have hamstring strains.

Conditioning and Injury Prevention

Conditioning and injury prevention are among the most important parts of athletic trainers' jobs. Athletic trainers help athletes stay in good condition to prevent injuries. They may work with athletes to develop exercise routines and healthy eating habits. Athletic trainers often help athletes perform warm-up exercises before competitions. These exercises reduce athletes' chances of suffering injuries such as muscle strains and cramps.

Athletic trainers prevent injuries in other ways. They may check playing surfaces and equipment before athletic events. They look for anything that could be dangerous to athletes. They report these hazards to athletes, coaches, and officials.

Rehabilitation

Athletic trainers help athletes recover from their injuries. This is called rehabilitation. Athletic trainers recommend rehabilitation

Athletic trainers may help athletes perform warm-up exercises before competitions.

programs. These programs include exercises that strengthen weakened muscles, tendons, and ligaments.

Athletic trainers sometimes use special equipment in their work. They use whirlpools to increase athletes' blood circulation. Good blood circulation helps injuries heal faster. Athletic trainers also use electrical stimulation equipment. Electrical stimulation aides in the healing of sprains and strains.

Work Environment

Athletic trainers work in many settings. Some work at colleges, universities, or high schools. These athletic trainers treat student athletes. Athletic trainers often must attend athletic events during evenings and weekends. Some athletic trainers in schools also teach classes.

Some athletic trainers work for professional sports teams. These trainers often work many hours during certain months when their teams train and compete. They sometimes travel with their teams.

Athletic trainers may help athletes exercise in fitness rooms.

Other athletic trainers work at clinics or for large companies. These athletic trainers may work daytime work hours. They may not have to provide immediate care at sporting events. They spend most of their time helping patients with conditioning, injury prevention, and rehabilitation.

Chapter 2

A Day on the Job

Athletic trainers perform many tasks each day. Their tasks and daily schedules depend on where they work. Many athletic trainers deal mainly with conditioning and injury prevention. Some mainly provide immediate care to injured athletes. Others concentrate on rehabilitation. But most athletic trainers do all of these tasks.

College and High School Sports

Athletic trainers at high schools, colleges, and universities work with members of student sports teams. They also work with other students. They may help these students create and follow exercise programs. These athletic trainers sometimes teach classes such as physical education.

Athletic trainers care for injuries athletes suffer during competitions.

Athletic trainers at schools perform various tasks throughout the day. They may spend their mornings working with students in rehabilitation rooms. They also may teach classes such as physical education. Athletic trainers at schools may spend their afternoons helping student athletes prepare for practices and competitions. They may work with athletes to help them stretch or condition. They sometimes meet with coaches to talk about student training programs.

Athletic trainers at schools may spend evenings at athletic events. Before competitions, they may tape athletes' ankles and wrists with athletic tape. This provides extra support to muscles and ligaments. During competitions, athletic trainers may provide immediate care to injured athletes.

Professional Sports

Athletic trainers with professional sports teams usually work for only one team. During competitions, they provide immediate care. These athletic trainers often see the same

Athletic trainers may work in rehabilitation rooms.

An athletic trainer may rush onto a playing field to treat an injured athlete.

kinds of injuries. For example, an athletic trainer on a football team may treat many strained hamstrings.

Athletic trainers on sports teams often work closely with coaches. Coaches want their players to remain healthy and free of injury. Coaches may want to be sure certain players are healthy for important games. For example, some baseball pitchers play about every five days. Athletic trainers help pitchers stay ready to perform when it is their turn to pitch.

Athletic trainers also work with athletes during the off season. Teams do not compete during this time. Athletic trainers help athletes with exercise programs and diets during the off season. They also help with long-term rehabilitation of athletes who have suffered serious injuries. Long-term rehabilitation may take months or even years. Athletic trainers also check athletes' health before the athletes begin their seasons.

Clinics

Some athletic trainers work at clinics. These athletic trainers mainly help athletes and other people rehabilitate. Sports teams may send players to clinics for rehabilitation. Most trainers at clinics see patients by appointment.

Athletic trainers at clinics help patients create and follow exercise programs. They may create programs that strengthen damaged muscles, ligaments, or tendons. These athletic trainers may work with physical therapists or occupational therapists to create exercise programs. Physical therapists and occupational therapists specialize in rehabilitation.

Companies
Some companies hire athletic trainers to help keep their employees in good physical condition. These athletic trainers may be in charge of company gymnasiums or exercise rooms. They often help employees follow exercise programs. These athletic trainers may lead exercise classes. These classes help workers stay healthy and productive.

Athletic trainers at companies may treat injuries that other athletic trainers do not. Employees who work in offices may have back pain from sitting all day. They may have pain in their hands and wrists from working at computers. Factory workers may suffer injuries from performing repetitive tasks. Athletic trainers must help these employees with injury prevention and rehabilitation. They provide treatments and exercises to prevent and heal injuries.

High School and College
Athletic trainers in schools provide conditioning and rehabilitation to student athletes. They also provide immediate care at sporting events. They need good decision-making skills to do this.

Professional Sports
Athletic trainers in professional sports provide immediate care during competitions. They also help athletes with conditioning, rehabilitation, and prevention. A specialized knowledge of a certain sport is helpful for this career.

Clinics
Athletic trainers in clinics mainly provide rehabilitation to athletes and other people. They need to know how to strengthen injured muscles, tendons, and ligaments.

Companies
Athletic trainers at private companies provide rehabilitation and conditioning to company employees. They prevent and treat job-related injuries. They should understand the special health concerns for workers in a variety of work environments.

Chapter 3

The Right Candidate

Athletic trainers need both social skills and technical skills. They should enjoy working with people. They should communicate clearly and listen well. They also must know how to treat many different injuries.

Interests

Athletic trainers should be interested in sports. They must understand which kinds of injuries are common to each sport. They must be prepared to treat these injuries. Athletic trainers also should understand the dangers of each sport. They must know how to prevent injuries common to each sport.

Athletic trainers must be interested in helping people. They should enjoy working with others.

Athletic trainers must understand the kinds of injuries that are common to each sport.

They spend many hours conditioning and rehabilitating athletes. This can be difficult work for both athletic trainers and athletes.

Abilities and Skills

Athletic trainers must be able to act quickly. They need good decision-making skills. They have to make decisions quickly when athletes are injured during competitions. Athletes' careers and even their lives may be at risk.

Athletic trainers must be able to handle stress. They are responsible for athletes' well-being. They may have to make decisions that permanently affect athletes' lives. Coaches and athletes may not like the decisions athletic trainers make. Athletic trainers must not allow this pressure to affect the treatment they provide.

Athletic trainers must know how to treat many different injuries. They must understand the human body and how muscles, ligaments, and tendons work together. They use this knowledge to recommend treatments and exercise programs.

Athletic trainers must be able to make quick decisions.

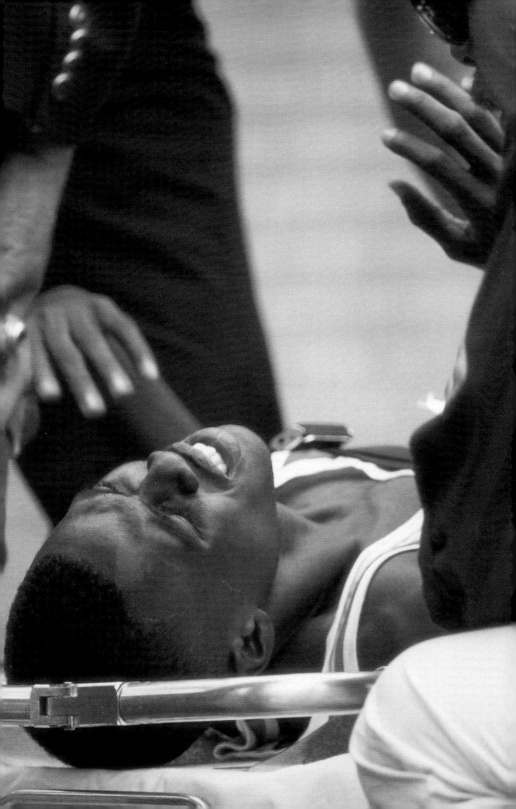

Skills

Workplace Skills   Yes / No

Resources:

Assign use of time . . . . ✓ | ☑
Assign use of money . . . . ☑ | ✓
Assign use of material and facility resources . . . . . ☑ |
Assign use of human resources . . . . ☑ |

Interpersonal Skills:

Take part as a member of a team . . . . ✓ |
Teach others . . . . ✓ |
Serve clients/customers . . . . ✓ |
Show leadership . . . . ✓ |
Work with others to arrive at a decision . . . . . . ✓ |
Work with a variety of people . . . . ✓ |

Information:

Acquire and judge information . . . . ✓ |
Understand and follow legal requirements . . . . ✓ |
Organize and maintain information . . . . . . ✓ |
Understand and communicate information . . . . ✓ |
Use computers to process information . . . . . ✓ |

Systems:

Identify, understand, and work with systems . . . . ✓ |
Understand environmental, social, political, economic,
    or business systems . . . . | ✓
Oversee and correct system performance . . . . . | ✓
Improve and create systems . . . . | ✓

Technology:

Select technology . . . . ✓ |
Apply technology to task . . . . ✓ |
Maintain and troubleshoot technology . . . . . . | ✓

Foundation Skills

Basic Skills:

Read . . . . ✓ |
Write . . . . ✓ |
Do arithmetic and math . . . . ✓ |
Speak and listen . . . . ✓ |

Thinking Skills:

Learn . . . . ✓ |
Reason . . . . ✓ |
Think creatively . . . . ✓ |
Make decisions . . . . ✓ |
Solve problems . . . . ✓ |

Personal Qualities:

Take individual responsibility . . . . ✓ |
Have self-esteem and self-management . . . . . . ✓ |
Be sociable . . . . ✓ |
Be fair, honest, and sincere . . . . ✓ |

Athletic trainers must work well with people. They may have to work with different personalities each day. They must get along with the athletes they treat. They need to earn athletes' trust. Athletic trainers sometimes must give athletes bad news about injuries. They must be caring and understanding. But they also must be firm with athletes. Athletes must follow athletic trainers' instructions in order to get better.

Communication skills also are important to athletic trainers. Athletic trainers provide important information to athletes, coaches, and doctors. They must be able to explain complex injuries and treatments clearly. Athletic trainers also must write and read well. They may have to read or write articles about athletic training in books and journals. This helps them keep up with the latest news in their field.

Athletic trainers should have computer skills. Some athletic trainers keep medical records on computers. Athletic trainers also may use the Internet to keep up with news in athletic training.

Chapter 4

Preparing for the Career

Athletic trainers must earn a bachelor's degree from a college or university. Most students earn this degree in about four years. A bachelor's degree prepares a student for certification as an athletic trainer. Certification is the official recognition of an athletic trainer's abilities. All athletic trainers in the United States and Canada must be certified.

High School Education

High school students interested in careers as athletic trainers should take science classes. Health, biology, and chemistry classes prepare

Students who want to become athletic trainers should take science classes.

students for athletic training programs in college. High school students also should learn first aid basics and CPR.

Other programs may help high school students learn more about athletic training. Students may try out for sports teams. This helps them understand athletes and competition. They may offer to work in youth sports programs. High school students can serve as coaches or officials for these programs. Students also may train to become lifeguards at swimming pools or beaches. This helps them learn about immediate care and other skills. Students may volunteer as student athletic trainers. They gain experience by helping professional athletic trainers.

Post-Secondary Education

Athletic trainers must have a bachelor's degree. Many colleges and universities offer this degree in athletic training. Students in athletic training programs take science classes. These

High school students interested in careers as athletic trainers should learn CPR.

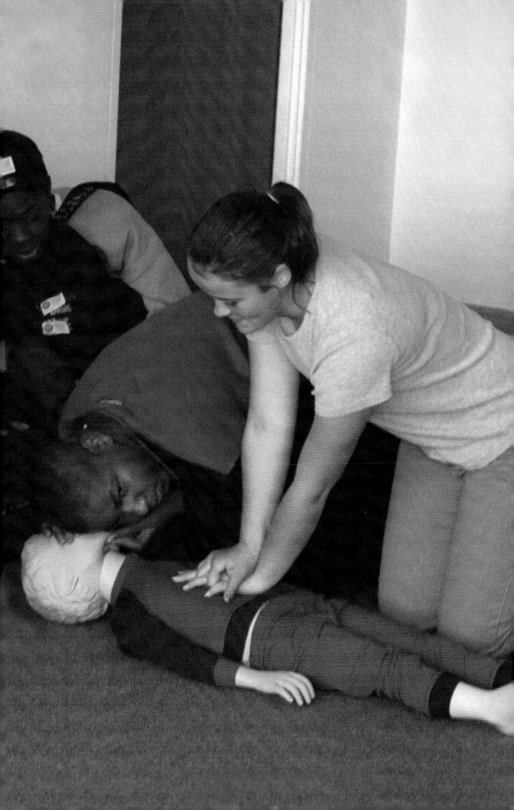

| High School Diploma | Bachelor's Degree |

usually include anatomy, physiology, and biomechanics. These sciences study the human body and how it moves.

Students of athletic training also take a variety of other classes. They may take psychology or coaching classes. These classes teach students to understand how coaches and athletes think. Students take classes on fitness and nutrition. Other classes teach students how to care for athletic injuries.

Students in athletic training programs usually work in college or university athletic or physical education departments. They may assist certified athletic trainers. This work prepares them for their careers. It also helps them prepare for certification tests.

Certification → Licensing (varies by state and province) →

Certification

Athletic trainers in the United States must be certified by the National Athletic Trainers' Association Board of Certification. In Canada, athletic therapists must be certified by the Canadian Athletic Therapists Association. These organizations set standards of ability for all athletic trainers and athletic therapists.

Graduates of athletic training programs must pass a written test to become certified. The test includes questions about emergency care, treatment methods, and rehabilitation. Graduates also must complete a practical. This test demonstrates hands-on skills.

Some states and provinces also require athletic trainers and athletic therapists to be licensed. Athletic trainers and athletic therapists may have to pass more tests to become licensed. The states or provinces write these tests.

Continuing Education

An athletic trainer's education does not end with certification. Certified athletic trainers must continue learning. They may take college classes and attend conferences to do this. They may learn about new treatment methods at these conferences and classes. They also can discuss trends in athletic training with other athletic trainers.

Many athletic trainers earn a master's degree. This degree usually requires one to three additional years of education. Students working on a master's degree study and research a particular area of athletic training. Athletic trainers who earn a master's degree often earn higher salaries than those who do not.

Some athletic trainers go back to school to earn a master's degree.

Chapter 5

The Market

The job market for athletic trainers is uncertain. This job market grew during the 1990s because many people became interested in fitness. Companies hired athletic trainers as a service to employees. College and professional sports also became more popular than ever. New sports teams created more jobs for athletic trainers. But experts do not expect this growth to continue. Experts predict that the job market for athletic trainers will remain about the same as it is now.

Salary

Most full-time athletic trainers in the United States earn between $17,000 and $30,000 per year. Most athletic therapists in Canada earn between $20,000 and $32,000.

Many athletic trainers found jobs in college and professional sports during the 1990s.

Athletic trainers can earn much more money by taking jobs with professional sports teams. These athletic trainers can earn as much as $200,000 per year.

Job Outlook

The job outlook for athletic trainers is uncertain. Many new athletic trainers entered the field during the 1990s. This led to increased competition for jobs. This competition may prevent athletic trainers from finding full-time jobs. Jobs in Canada may be especially hard to find.

Athletic trainers in the United States may have the greatest chance of finding jobs at high schools. Some states have passed laws that require full-time athletic trainers at high schools. This has led to an increase in job openings.

Job openings with colleges, professional sports teams, and clinics are expected to stay about the same. There is a great deal of competition in the United States and Canada for these job openings.

Athletic trainers in the United States may have the greatest chance of finding jobs in high schools.

Advancement

Athletic trainers advance by gaining experience and knowledge. Athletic trainers at clinics may be given more responsibilities as they gain experience. Athletic trainers in high schools may find jobs with college athletic programs. They then may advance to jobs with professional sports teams.

Athletic trainers work with many others in the sports medicine field. They work with physical therapists, occupational therapists, nutritionists, and doctors. These professionals work together to make sure athletes receive the best care possible.

Athletic trainers need training and knowledge to find jobs.

Words to Know

anatomy (uh-NAT-uh-mee)—the study of the human body

biomechanics (bye-oh-muh-KA-niks)—the study of how the human body moves

certification (sur-ti-fuh-KAY-shun)—official recognition of a person's abilities

concussion (kuhn-KUSH-uhn)—an injury to the brain from a hard blow to the head

ligament (LIG-uh-muhnt)—a band of tissue that connects one bone to another

physiology (fiz-ee-OL-uh-jee)—the study of how the human body works

sprain (SPRAYN)—a stretch or tear of a ligament

strain (STRAYN)—a stretch or tear of a muscle or tendon

tendon (TEN-duhn)—a band of tissue that connects a muscle to a bone

To Learn More

Cosgrove, Holli, ed. *Career Discovery Encyclopedia. Vol. 1.* Chicago: Ferguson Publishing, 2000.

Fischer, David K. *The 50 Coolest Jobs in Sports: Who's Got Them, What They Do, and How You Can Get One!* New York: Macmillan, 1997.

Heitzmann, William Ray. *Careers for Sports Nuts & Other Athletic Types.* VGM Careers for You. Lincolnwood, Ill.: VGM Career Horizons, 1997.

Lee, Barbara. *Working in Sports and Recreation.* Exploring Careers. Minneapolis: Lerner Publications, 1996.

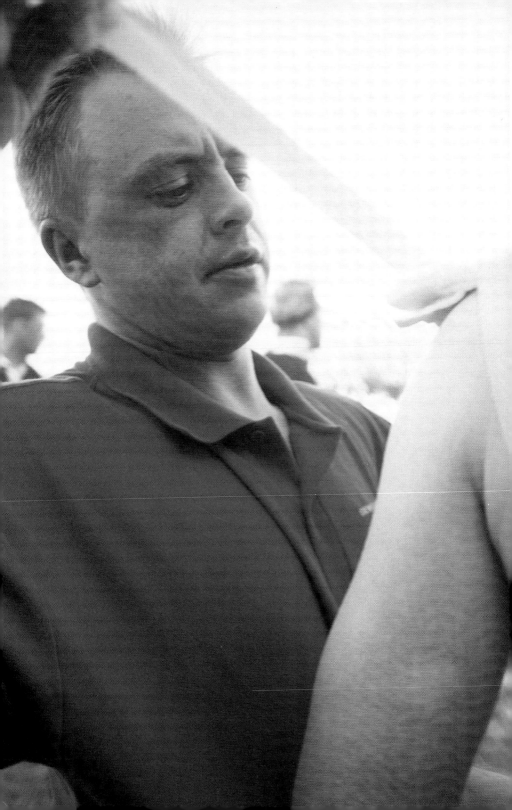

Useful Addresses

Canadian Athletic Therapists Association
902 11th Avenue SW
Suite 312
Calgary, AB T2R 0E7
Canada

National Athletic Trainers' Association
2952 Stemmons Freeway
Dallas, TX 75247-6196

National Youth Sports Safety Foundation
333 Longwood Avenue
Suite 202
Boston, MA 02115

Internet Sites

Canadian Athletic Therapists Association
http://www.mtroyal.ab.ca/CATA/splash.html

**MSPWeb Sports Medicine Related
   Organizations**
http://www.mspweb.com/orgs.html

National Athletic Trainers' Association
http://www.nata.org

National Youth Sports Safety Foundation
http://www.nyssf.org/welcome.html